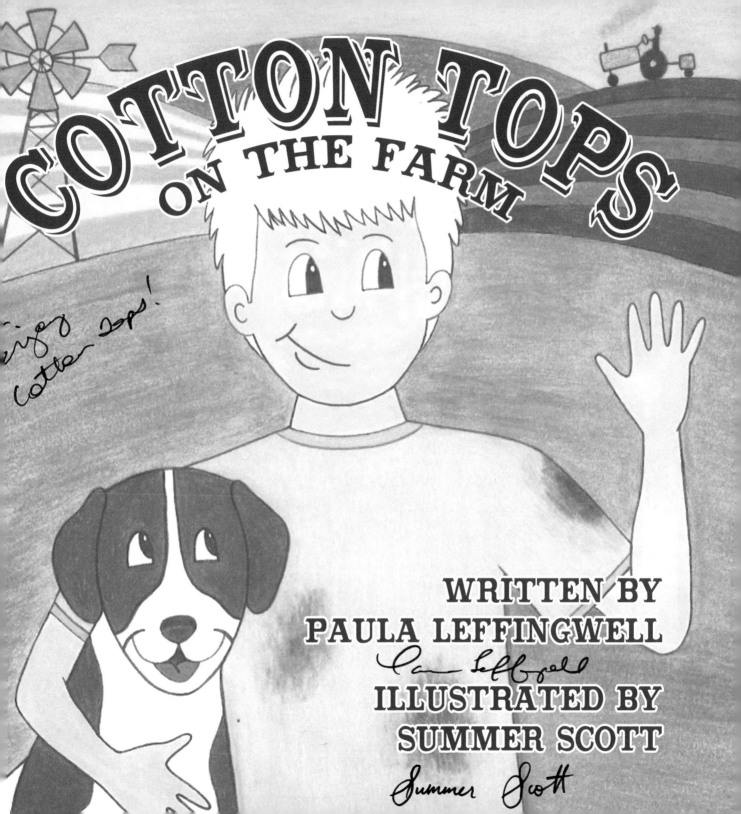

In memory of Rodney,
the real Cotton Tops

This Book Belongs to

Tristen
_____

Many years ago, there was a blond-haired, blue-eyed little boy who grew up on a farm in Oklahoma.

This little boy's hair was so white and stood up so tall that all his friends called him Cotton Tops. Cotton Tops didn't care what they called him; all he cared about was the farm he lived on. This was a big farm with cows, horses, goats, peacocks, and roosters.

This farm also had one big barn and one big shed. Cotton Tops loved everything about this farm. He would spend all day outside and come inside at night dirty as a pig.

His dad, Farmer Henry, taught him how to do all the work to make h.
farm successful. Cotton Tops was by his dad's side all day long workir
on the farm. When Cotton Tops got older, he did all the farming himsel

Cotton Tops planted wheat in the fall so it could grow in the spring. Year after year, crops of wheat were planted.

He planted the wheat in perfect rows with his tractor and his drill. With the sun and the rain, the wheat grew to be very tall.

When the wheat had grown enough, Cotton
Tops harvested it with his combine.

Cotton Tops also bought many, many cows. He would water and fee
them every day. When some of the older cows had baby calves, Cotto
Tops would keep them close to his house.

He fed them with a bottle
and kept them warm when
it was cold.

When they were strong enough to be on their own, the baby calves would go back out to pasture to be with the other cows. The other cows taught them how to eat grass and live a happy cow life.

otton Tops also had a few horses and a few goats. The horses stayed
ut in the pasture, but the goats hung out around the house. Cotton Tops
ked to have the goats around because they ate weeds in the grass.

Besides cows, horses, and goats, Cotton Tops' farm also had peacocks and roosters. The peacocks would roam the farm and add beauty to it with their colorful feathers. The roosters crowed early in the morning to let him know it was time to go to work.

COCK-A-DOODLE DOO

Cotton Tops worked on his farm before the sun came up and kept working until after the sun went down. Everyone who passed by his fields bragged about how great the crops looked and how clean his farm was.

Cotton Tops was proud. Nothing made him happier than his farm and everything on it. He soon became known as the best farmer in the county. All the other farmers were jealous of Cotton Tops and his farming methods.

But no matter what the other farmers thought,
Cotton Tops kept on farming.

And he kept on raising cows, horses and goats........

And he kept letting the peacocks roam the land freely......

And the roosters kept waking him every morning so he could get to work.

COCK-A-DOODLE DOO

And no one ever made fun of his name, Cotton Tops, because they grew to respect him for the excellent farmer he was.

CPSIA information can be obtained
at www.ICGtesting.com
Printed in the USA
LVHW07n0149300918
591885LV00001B/1/P